What Happens While You Sleep

Anna Russelmann & Judith Buchner

Translated by David Henry Wilson

FAIRY TALE

North South

Today was a lovely day! Malu went to the zoo with her parents. In the afternoon she did some painting and played in the garden, and in the evening Mom made some pancakes—yummy!

Now it's bedtime, but Malu is not in the least bit tired. She would prefer to have something to drink and look at a book or play with her building blocks.

But where is Teddy? Without her favorite cuddly toy, Malu can't go to sleep anyway.

She looks everywhere—among
her toys and under the pillow—but
there's no sign of the little bear. Then
Malu lies on her bed and has a good think
about where else Teddy might be.
As she lies there, she starts to yawn
and feel really sleepy.

But what actually happens in our heads, or to be more precise in our brains, when we sleep? Nothing? Oh no, lots of things happen!

Can you see Conshus up there in her watchtower? Conshus is a real thinker. It doesn't matter what Malu does, she's always thinking at the same time. And so of course she's been thinking about where Teddy might be hiding and looking through her binoculars to try and find him. But now she looks behind her at her time-ball.

"Oh, it's time I was asleep!"

Conshus closes the shutters,
turns out the light, and goes to bed.
Meanwhile, Malu's eyes have
closed and now she is asleep.

Everything is dark in the tower. But far down below, in a little hollow, it suddenly becomes very bright. This is the sorting office—a very important place. Because everything that Malu experienced during the day ends up here, to be sorted and stored.

That is the job of Hippo and Campus, the heroes of our story. They are at home here, and this is the time when they really come to life. With eager curiosity they collect the evening mail.

Hippo fetches the packages that have come by air and also picks up a postcard.

In the meantime, Campus attends to the messages in bottles. He patiently fishes the last bottle out of the water, then goes back to the sorting office.

This is the mail for a single day! Hippo and Campus are amazed. Malu has experienced all this today!

When Malu sees, hears, smells, touches, thinks, or does anything, it ends up here in her brain. And Hippo and Campus will sort out all these different impressions tonight.

Malu saw this beautiful butterfly in the garden today. Hippo hangs the picture in a frame on the wall. From now on, Malu will know exactly what a butterfly looks like.

Campus opens the first bottled mail. Ooooh! The delicious smell of pancakes comes wafting out of the bottle. That was the evening treat, with cinnamon and sugar. From now on, pancakes will be Malu's favorite food.

Campus puts the bottle in the treasure chest.
This is where all the favorite things are safely stored.

Now Hippo takes a photo out of an envelope.

"This is Malu with the elephants in the zoo," says
Hippo enthusiastically. "Oh, it was lovely this morning
with Mom and Dad."

"Yes, that was a great moment," Campus agrees.
Something like that also has to go in the treasure chest
so that Malu can keep remembering it for a long time.

Hippo unrolls a large sheet of paper. "Malu painted this herself! She wrote her name on it several times and then crossed it out again."

"Aha! That's the way you have to write the letter *L*," Campus observes. As Malu learned that today, it has to replace the inverted *L* in the tree of knowledge.

Hippo and Campus make their way to the tree, where there are a few letters and numbers hanging from the branches. These are the ones that Malu already knows.

There's plenty of room here for everything that she will learn in the future.
And wherever something is added,
new leaves and branches grow.

Since Malu had lots of different experiences today, Hippo and Campus have piles of mail to sort out and put away neatly or to discard.

This is important, because it will leave plenty of space for all the new things that tomorrow will bring.

But of course, all this sorting takes time and so Hippo and Campus are pleased when Malu goes to bed early.

They've already achieved a lot, and now they
allow themselves to have a breather.

"What should we do about the bicycle?" asks Hippo.
When Malu was practicing riding it today, she fell off.
"She's sure to try again tomorrow," says Campus.
"Then we'd better keep it for the moment," decides Hippo.

Hippo and Campus only keep things that will be important or useful for the future. They remove the rest of the mail and put it in the garbage can. That's why they only hold on to one of the countless pictures of daisies. Malu finds it boring to remember the same thing over and over again. And it's boring anyway to keep hearing "Maluhu! Tidy up!"

Wait! What's that lying over there? An important photo,
and they were just about to throw it away!

"It's Teddy!" cries Hippo in surprise. "She must have had him with her in the bathroom when she brushed her teeth and then forgotten."

Campus has an idea: "We'll take the photo to Conshus in the watchtower. Then tomorrow morning when she wakes up, Malu will remember where she left her little bear."

But the sheer amount of work has made the time pass very quickly. Soon the night will be over. That can be seen from the time-ball at the top of the tower.

Hippo notices it and starts to get agitated. "Oh dear! Time's moving fast! Malu will be waking up soon! We must hurry! Come on!"

"Wait! It'll be quicker by bike," says Campus. "Okay, you steer, and I'll hold on to you," replies Hippo.

"Wheeeee!"

When they arrive at the tower,
Campus is completely out of breath.
"How are we going to get up it?" he pants.
Hippo grins. "By airmail, of course.
I think we've got a package left.
We can use the balloons."
"Okay, but you do the flying."
Campus unties the balloons and
takes hold of Hippo's hand.

At this moment,
the new day dawns
on the time-ball.

Conshus yawns
and stretches…

…opens the shutters,
and can hardly believe
her eyes!

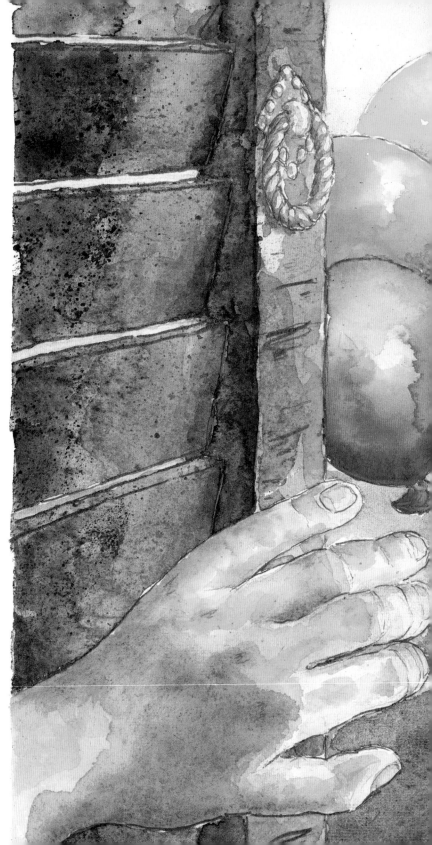

In front of her
is Hippo in midair,
frantically waving
a photograph.

Suddenly there's a loud noise....

Malu wakes up with a start. "What was that noise? Was it a dream?"

But then she sees that her pink balloon has burst. She sees a picture before her eyes: Teddy on the toilet paper roll! She hurries as fast as she can to the bathroom.

"There you are, Teddy!"she shouts, and gives her cuddly little bear a big, happy hug. Together again, the two of them prepare for a new day.

You see, lots of things happen while we're asleep.

What new adventures will Malu's little helpers have tonight?